# SAINT FRANCIS AND THE ANIMALS

## A MOTHER BIRD'S STORY

## PHIL GALLERY

### ILLUSTRATED BY
## SIBYL MACKENZIE

San Damiano Books
PARACLETE PRESS

BREWSTER, MASSACHUSETTS

With gratitude, this book is dedicated to Father Patrick Adams,
Father Gordian Vincent Ehrlacher, Father Bo McMillan, and Father Ray Bean.
All were members of the Order of Friars Minor, called Franciscans. I was
blessed to have them as guides as I moved from childhood to adulthood.
May they rest in peace.

— PHIL GALLERY

2018 First printing

*Saint Francis and the Animals*

Text copyright © 2018 by Phil Gallery
Illustrations copyright © 2018 by Sibyl MacKenzie

ISBN 978-1-61261-973-6

The Paraclete Press name and logo (dove on cross) are trademarks of Paraclete Press, Inc.

Library of Congress Cataloging-in-Publication Data
Names: Gallery, Philip D., author.
Title: St. Francis and the animals : a mother bird's story / Phil Gallery ;
   illustrated by Sibyl MacKenzie.
Description: Brewster, MA : Paraclete Press, Inc., 2018.
Identifiers: LCCN 2018014704 | ISBN 9781612619736 (hardcover sc)
Subjects:  LCSH: Francis, of Assisi, Saint, 1182-1226—Juvenile literature.
Classification: LCC BX4700.F69 G35 2018 | DDC 271/.302—dc23
LC record available at https://lccn.loc.gov/2018014704

10 9 8 7 6 5 4 3 2 1

Published by Paraclete Press
Brewster, Massachusetts
www.paracletepress.com

Printed in the United States of America

## NOTE TO PARENTS, TEACHERS, AND ADULTS WHO READ THIS BOOK WITH CHILDREN

We live in a world cluttered with sights and sounds. Our eyes and ears are so bombarded, we can become blind and deaf to the natural sights and sounds of God's Creation.

Saint Francis was a man who paid close attention to Creation. As he walked through the woods, he talked to the animals, addressing them as his "brothers" and "sisters." Looking at a tree, he might say, "Thank you, Brother Tree, for the shade you give me in the summer and for the fruit you give me to eat. Thank you for your branches where my sister birds can build their homes, and for the wood we use to heat our homes and cook our food."

He called the sun his brother and the moon his sister. Francis used all his senses to help him appreciate God's world. The more he became involved with nature, the closer he felt to God. But because he talked to animals, many people thought Francis had lost his senses—that he had "gone crazy." Nothing could have been further from the truth.

Saint Francis could hear the voice of God, which told him that God loved him. Knowing he was loved by God filled Francis with gratitude and happiness.

This book is a look at how this gratitude and happiness led Francis to treat his brother and sister creatures with respect. It offers a vision for the many ways that all of us, humans and other animals and all of Creation, are connected parts of God's world. For the young children with whom you read this book, talking to animals and trees will probably make perfect sense. Here's hoping you will encourage them to do so.

The big day for Benjamin Bird's first flight had arrived. "May I go now, Mother?" he asked.

"No, my dear. Before you go, I must tell you the story of our human friend. His name is Brother Francis."

"Do you have to?" asked Benjamin.

"Yes, my son," answered Mother Bird. "And you must remember every word, because one day you must tell your children the story."

So Mother Bird began her wondrous tale. "Our friend, Brother Francis, was born in the nearby town of Assisi."

"When Brother Francis was a young boy," Mother Bird continued, "he was kind and generous and had many friends."

"Will I have lots of friends, Mother?" asked Benjamin Bird.

"Yes," answered Mother Bird, "if you are kind and generous. Now, Benjamin," Mother Bird added gently, "I must get on with my story.

"Francis's father was a rich man and he gave him many things, including a brave and beautiful horse. When our friend was young, he loved to dress in colorful clothes and ride his horse through the countryside around Assisi. He would play his mandolin and sing songs about heroic adventure. He dreamed that one day he would be a hero and people would sing songs about him."

"But then one day Brother Francis rode his brave horse out of Assisi in search of adventure."

"What kind of adventure, Mother?"

"He was going to join an army in places he did not yet know. Remember, Benjamin, he wanted to be a hero. But on the way, the Maker of All Things told him to return home. Our friend was sad because he thought he was never going to become a great hero. Brother Francis felt sad and uncertain. What would he do, now? But by the time he got home, Francis wasn't sad anymore. He patted Brother Horse and thanked him for helping him to feel better."

## FRANCIS MEETS THE BIRDS

Mother Bird paused. Benjamin Bird flapped his wings. "A horse and a man can't be brothers," he said, scratching his head.

"Brother Francis says we are all brothers and sisters, my dear," answered Mother Bird. "Just listen," she said, and continued her tale.

"One day, while walking down a road with his friends, Brother Francis noticed that the woods were full of all kinds of birds. He left his companions and ran into the woods. The birds watched as he ran toward them, but not one bird moved. When Francis was in the middle of the birds, he began to talk to them."

"But, Mother, people don't do that. People don't talk with us," Benjamin Bird said, as he looked at all the birds gathering in the trees around them.

"Brother Francis did, my dear."

# BIRDS FLY TO BROTHER FRANCIS

"Our friend told our brother and sister birds that they must always thank God for the feathers he gave them to wear, and the wings he gave them to fly. As Brother Francis was speaking, the birds flew to him. Some landed on the ground nearby, and some landed on his arms and head. Then he told our brother and sister birds to fly off into the sky that God has given them for their home, and to be joyful."

"Wait, Mother. Please tell me who is God?" asked Benjamin Bird.

"God is the Maker of All Things," answered Mother Bird.

# FRANCIS AND THE FISHERMAN

"May I try flying now, Mother?" asked Benjamin, hopping up and down with excitement.

"Not yet. I must finish my story first," she said.

She continued: "One day, Brother Francis met a fisherman who had just caught a fish. Our friend asked the fisherman to give him the fish. The fisherman did.

"Then, Francis addressed Brother Fish with love and concern, saying, 'Be more careful and try not to get caught again.' Then he gently put the fish back in the water, and the fish swam away."

# FRANCIS RELEASES A TRAPPED RABBIT

"One sunny, summer day, Brother Francis was walking in the woods and he heard a weak, sad sound coming from among the trees. He followed the sound and found a small rabbit whose foot was caught in a trap. Francis knelt next to the frightened bunny and gently released her leg from the awful trap. He held Sister Rabbit in his hands and told her she too must be more careful.

"When he was finished talking to Sister Rabbit, he laid her on the ground. But she jumped right back into his arms. So then, Francis walked deeper into the woods, set her down again, and she hopped away."

Benjamin Bird flapped his wings. "Is your story over now, Mother?" he asked.

"Almost, my dear. I have one more tale to tell."

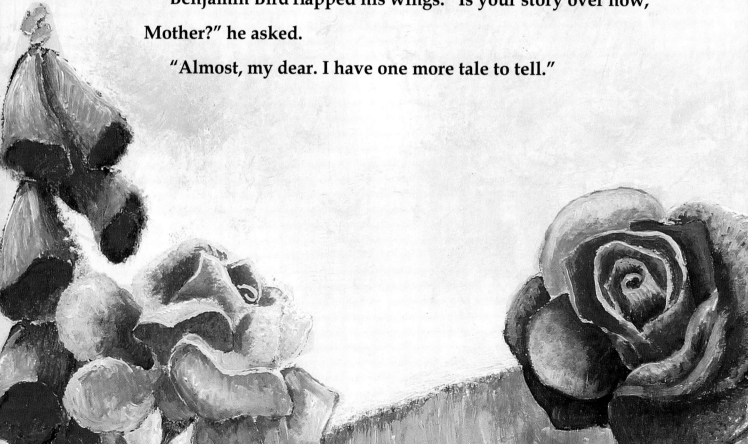

Before Mother Bird could continue, Father Bird landed in the nest with a snack for his son.

Benjamin finished the snack quickly. He was hungry! Then, Mother Bird continued.

"Once a very mean and scary wolf lived near a small town and was attacking the people's animals. Then, he even began attacking the people.

"The townspeople did not know what to do. They told Brother Francis about the scary wolf, and Francis agreed to go out from the city to find this Brother Wolf."

"Our friend must be very brave," said Benjamin Bird. Mother Bird smiled and nodded her head.

# BROTHER WOLF CHARGES FRANCIS

"Suddenly the wolf charged from the woods," Mother Bird continued.

"Oh my!" cried Benjamin Bird.

"Brother Wolf was heading right at Brother Francis," said Mother Bird. "Our friend ordered the wolf to stop and listen to him. Brother Wolf stopped and listened. Then, Francis asked Brother Wolf why he was harming the people's animals, and why sometimes he even attacked the people."

# FRANCIS AND BROTHER WOLF MAKE A DEAL

"Brother Francis asked Brother Wolf to come to him," Mother Bird continued.

"Oh no!" cried Benjamin Bird.

"Yes, my son," she went on, "the wolf came and sat in front of our friend. Brother Francis petted the wolf's chest and told him he must never again hurt the people because they are made in the image of God. Brother Wolf nodded his head. Then he licked Francis's hand.

"Then, my dear, our friend told Brother Wolf to follow him into town, where he would help Brother Wolf make peace with the people."

"Oh my," Benjamin Bird said. "Oh my."

# BENJAMIN BIRD TAKES TO THE SKY

"Now my story of Saint Francis is finished, my son," said Mother Bird.

"Do you think I will ever meet him, Mother?" asked Benjamin Bird.

"I hope so, dear. But few of us have been lucky enough to see him."

"I want to see Brother Francis one day."

"I do too," she replied, "but now the time has come for you to fly into the home God has given us."

"I'm ready," said Benjamin Bird, as he stood on the edge of the nest and tested his wings. Mother and Father held their breath. Benjamin leaped into the sky.

# BENJAMIN BIRD CRASHES AT THE FEET OF A HOODED MAN

At first, things went well. Benjamin Bird flew higher and higher. But when he looked down and saw all the animals on the ground and how high he was, he became frightened. He began to flap his wings wildly as he began to fall back to earth. Down and down he fell, flapping one way then another. His mother and father were close behind him, but there was nothing they could do. He would have to learn how to fly on his own.

Before Benjamin Bird hit the ground, he spread his wings and crashed into a pile of leaves. Looking up from the pile, he saw that he was at the feet of a human dressed in a long robe with a hood over his head.

# FRANCIS SPEAKS

Brother Francis removed his hood, reached down, and picked up Benjamin Bird. "Don't be afraid," he said. "I am your friend. I am Brother Francis. God has given you beautiful wings to fly. Soon you will learn how to use them."

Other animals were around them, and they began to talk excitedly to one another, saying, "It is our friend! It is Brother Francis!"

Francis said to them: "Sisters and brothers, I hope you will always thank God for the gifts he has given you. And love one another as God loves you. I ask God's blessings for every one of you. Thank you for your friendship and for the help you have given me on my journey with God."

Then, Francis gently tossed Benjamin Bird into the air, and turned and walked into the woods, just as Benjamin Bird rose confidently into the sky.

# ANOTHER BIRD PREPARES TO FLY

High in the branches of a nearby tree a young bird began to flap her wings. Her parents looked lovingly at her as she prepared to take her first flight.

"The time has come," said Father Bird, "to tell her the story of our friend before she flies into the home God has given her in sky."

"Can I please fly, now?" Bella Bird asked.

"Not yet, dear," answered Mother Bird. Then, Father Bird hopped to his daughter's side. "First, we must tell you the tale of our friend Brother Francis," he said. "Francis was born in the nearby town of Assisi. He spent his life teaching all living things that we are brothers and sisters because we are all made by God."